The Tale of Captain

Blackstrap Molasses

Fulton Books, Inc.
Meadville, PA

Published by Fulton Books 2020

ISBN 978-1-64654-788-3 (paperback)
ISBN 978-1-64654-789-0 (digital)

Printed in the United States of America

The Tale of Captain

Blackstrap Molasses

C. J. Perkins

Long, long ago in the sweetest of seas lived Captain Blackstrap Molasses. She ran her ship fiercely with her sugarcane by her side and her gingerbread men as her crew.

No amount of syrup or honey could hold the captain back from those sweet seas.

One blustery day, the captain and crew sailed off from Flour and Salt Island. The day was young when a cinnamon spice and everything nice, bake storm poured down on Captain Blackstrap Molasses and her crew. Baking Soda poured in from the east. Cinnamon poured in from the west, Ginger poured in from the south, and Cloves came from the north.

Soon the seas became smooth, and Captain Blackstrap

Molasses was back in control of her ship.

One of the gingerbread men shouted with excitement, "Ahoy!"

Pirate Dairy was headed in their direction. What to do? The crew scrambled. Pirate Dairy shot an egg at their ship… and then…another…and then…butter! The seas began whipping uncontrollably, the ship spun away from Pirate Dairy.

Just when Captain Blackstrap Molasses thought the bake storm couldn't get any worse, there was a heavy downpour of sugar and molasses.

The ship came to a sudden halt, and they docked their ship. The captain and her crew went to explore the Refrigeration Station. It was very chilly.

They chilled there for an hour.

Back to the ship they went. After having such a rough morning at sea, the captain and her crew decided to play a game called "roll yourself in a ball and splash into a pool of sugar."

The weather was changing once again. The temperature was rising—quite quickly, to 375 degrees to be exact. The crew found the new weather relaxing. They relaxed in that warm place for eight to ten minutes.

The captain and her crew had enough of that heat. They felt toasty, so they sailed further east near the Wire Rack Cove.

Finally, the day was coming to an end for those on the sweetest of seas. The baking storm had ceased. Captain Blackstrap Molasses and her crew rested in the cove after a very busy day.

Recipes

Ginger Crinkles

1 1/2 c. butter or margarine
2 c. sugar
1/2 c. of molasses
2 eggs
4 c. of flour (half white / half wheat depending on taste)
2 tsp. baking soda
2 tsp. baking powder
1/2 tsp. cloves
2 tsp. ginger
2 tsp. cinnamon
1/4 c. ground flax seed
1 tsp. nutmeg
1/2 tsp. salt
1/2 tsp. allspice

Beat together butter and sugar. Beat in molasses and eggs until light and fluffy. Add dry ingredients and mix until smooth. Chill at least 1 hour. Form into walnut-sized balls and dip in sugar. Bake at 375 degrees for 8–10 minutes.

Gingerbread Boys

Cream together
    1 c. butter
    1 c. brown sugar
    2 eggs
    1 c. dark molasses

Mix together
    4 1/2 c. flour
    1 tsp. baking soda
    1 tsp. salt
    2 tsp. baking powder
    2 tsp. ginger
    1 tsp. allspice
    4 tsp. cinnamon
    1 tsp. ground orange peel
    1 tsp. cloves
    1 tsp. nutmeg

Add dry ingredients to creamed mixture, blend well. Chill at least 8 hours. Roll out to cut with cookie cutters. Bake at 350 degrees for 10–12 minutes. Decorate as desired.

About the Author

C. J. Perkins lives in Northeast Ohio with her handsome husband, T. J., and her energetic son, Rocco. C. J. didn't invent reading, writing, or arithmetic, but she's a big fan of reading and writing.

If you'd like to contact C. J., her e-mail address is captainblackstrapmolasses@outlook.com.

CPSIA information can be obtained
at www.ICGtesting.com
Printed in the USA
BVHW021540140721
611836BV00037B/1564